My Emotions

HAPPY

A Crabtree Roots Book

AMY CULLIFORD

CRABTREE
Publishing Company
www.crabtreebooks.com

School-to-Home Support for Caregivers and Teachers

This book helps children grow by letting them practice reading. Here are a few guiding questions to help the reader with building his or her comprehension skills. Possible answers appear here in red.

Before Reading:

- What do I think this book is about?
    - *This book is about feeling happy.*
    - *This book is about what feeling happy looks like.*

- What do I want to learn about this topic?
    - *I want to learn what makes me feel happy.*
    - *I want to learn what feeling happy looks like.*

During Reading:

- I wonder why...
    - *I wonder why we smile when we are happy.*
    - *I wonder why we jump when we are happy.*

- What have I learned so far?
    - *I have learned that playing makes me feel happy.*
    - *I have learned that people laugh when they are happy.*

After Reading:

- What details did I learn about this topic?
    - *I have learned that there are many things that can make people happy.*
    - *I have learned that there are many ways you can look when you feel happy.*

- Read the book again and look for the vocabulary words.
    - *I see the word **hugs** on page 4 and the word **friends** on page 8. The other vocabulary words are found on page 14.*

What makes me **happy**?

Hugs make
me happy.

I **smile** when I am happy.

Playing with **friends** makes me happy.

I **laugh** when I am happy.

Helping people
makes me happy.

I jump when I am happy.

What makes you happy?

Word List

Sight Words

am
I
jump
make
me
people
what
when
with
you

Words to Know

friends

happy

hugs

laugh

smile

41 Words

What makes me **happy**?

Hugs make me happy.

I **smile** when I am happy.

Playing with **friends** makes me happy.

I **laugh** when I am happy.

Helping people makes me happy.

I jump when I am happy.

What makes you happy?

CRABTREE Publishing Company

Written by: Amy Culliford
Designed by: Rhea Wallace
Series Development: James Earley
Proofreader: Ellen Rodger
Educational Consultant: Marie Lemke M.Ed.

Photographs:
Shutterstock: Juan Pablo Gonzaález: cover; Sergey Novikov: p. 1; Ami Parikh: p. 3, 14; pixelheadphoto: p. 5, 14; wavebreakmedia: p. 7, 14; ESBProfessional: p. 8, 14; TinnaPong: p. 9, 14; Africa Studio: p. 11; Monkey Business Images: p. 12; alexei_tm: p. 13

My Emotions

HAPPY

Library and Archives Canada Cataloguing in Publication

Title: Happy / Amy Culliford.
Names: Culliford, Amy, 1992- author.
Description: Series statement: My emotions | "A Crabtree roots book".
Identifiers: Canadiana (print) 20210156651 | Canadiana (ebook) 2021015666X | ISBN 9781427139658 (hardcover) | ISBN 9781427139719 (softcover) | ISBN 9781427133366 (HTML) | ISBN 9781427139771 (read-along ebook) | ISBN 9781427133960 (EPUB)
Subjects: LCSH: Happiness in children—Juvenile literature. | LCSH: Happiness—Juvenile literature.
Classification: LCC BF723.H37 C85 2021 | DDC j152.4/2—dc23

Library of Congress Cataloging-in-Publication Data

Names: Culliford, Amy, 1992- author.
Title: Happy / Amy Culliford.
Description: New York : Crabtree Publishing, 2021. | Series: My emotions, a crabtree roots book | Includes index.
Identifiers: LCCN 2021009516 (print) | LCCN 2021009517 (ebook) | ISBN 9781427139658 (hardcover) | ISBN 9781427139719 (paperback) | ISBN 9781427133366 (ebook) | ISBN 9781427133960 (epub) | ISBN 9781427139771 (read along)
Subjects: LCSH: Happiness in children--Juvenile literature.
Classification: LCC BF723.H37 C85 2021 (print) | LCC BF723. H37 (ebook) | DDC 155.4/19--dc23
LC record available at https://lccn.loc.gov/2021009516
LC ebook record available at https://lccn.loc.gov/2021009

Crabtree Publishing Company
www.crabtreebooks.com 1-800-387-7650

Printed in Canada/092022/CPC20220913

Published in the United States
Crabtree Publishing
347 Fifth Avenue, Suite 1402-145
New York, NY, 10016

Published in Canada
Crabtree Publishing
616 Welland Ave.
St. Catharines, Ontario L2M 5V6